# A Look

A collection of gothic po..., 

By Marcus A. B.-Andrews

Author's Note: At first, it was a hobby, but it began to grow on me. I collected books and magazines to inspire my work, but it was only till I bought my first insider's guide to the **Wizarding World of Harry Potter.** It *truly* inspired my poetry as I incorporated magic into everything I wrote. When I gained a membership to Barnes & Noble, I was welcomed to a whole new world of reading.

# Table of Contents

The Face in the Looking Glass
Page1

Song of Sorrows
Page2

Harmony for a Blackened Soul
Page3

Metal and Rock
Page4

Into my Mind
Page5

Beauty of Tragedies
Page6

My Inner Blackness
Page7

Art of the Aura
Page8

Under the Mask and In the Mirror
Page9

Poetry of a Madman
Page10

Journal of a Blackened Heart
Page11

Soul of the Wolf
Page12

The Last Sail of the Seaghoul
Page13

As Bats take Flight
Page14

Specter of the Dark Theater
Page15

Ghosts' Night Out
Page16

Down in Cryptsville
Page17

Secrets of Enigma Island
Page18

Shadows of Grim Jazz
Page19

Terror among the Fields
Page20

Along came a Spider
Page21

Nightmare under the Big Top
Page22

The Creation of a Monster
Page23

Boogeyman of the Bayou
Page24

The Dark Side of Comics
Page25

The Spirit of Fright on All Hollow's Night　　　　Page26

One Good Scare
Page27

Under the Tombstone
Page28

The Black Granite
Page29

Down for the Final Count
Page30

Madame of Blackness
Page31

Two States of the Same Mind　　　　Page32

Of Two Minds
Page33

When Two Minds become One　　　　Page34

A Mind Split in Two　　　　Page35

My Dark Reflection　　　　Page36

The Ways of You-Know-Who　　　　Page37

| | |
|---|---|
| Emperor of Entropy | Page38 |
| Hands and Sands | Page39 |
| The Grand Duke of Night | Page40 |
| Howl of the Hound | Page41 |
| The Isle of No Escape | Page42 |
| Welcome to the House of Bio-exorcism | Page43 |
| Legends beyond the Grave | Page44 |
| Pleasant Dreams, Pleasant Screams | Page45 |
| The Dark Side of Imagination | Page46 |
| My Dark Oz | Page47 |
| A Dark and Snowy Night | Page48 |
| A Sad and Blue Day | Page49 |
| Counting down the All Hollow's Clock | Page50 |
| Screams at Storytime | Page51 |

My Perilous Place
Page52

Zoo of the Nocturnal
Page53

Nursery of Nightmares                                    Page54

Fiendish Fools
Page55

Bloodsuckers' Ball
Page56

Phantoms of Mardi Gras                                   Page57

Old Wicked West                                          Page58

Last Ride at Sundown                                     Page59

Elemental Darkness                                       Page60

Winter Terrorland                                        Page61

A Spell from Down Below
Page62

Khristmas of Krampus
Page63

My Raging Elemental
Page64

Little Store of Nightmares
Page65

Council of Goth Lords
Page66

A Wayward Land
Page67

Nocturnal Horror
Page68

The Forsaken Island
Page69

The Silent Face of Tragedy
Page70

The Goblin Hour of Night
Page71

Dark Justice
Page72

A Harmonious Hex
Page73

Bewitched by the Bogeywoman
Page74

Land of Pitch Black
Page75

Wraith of the Witchdoctor
Page76

The Black Palace
Page77

His Royal Horrificness
Page78

A Spooktacular Sundown
Page79

Lord of the Unliving
Page80

The Dark Baron of Bats            Page81

Shades and Contrasts of Night     Page82

Frightmare Night
Page83

The Origin of a Dark Professor
Page84

Chiroptophobia
Page85

Shades of Blackened Blue
Page86

Shades of Darkened Purple
Page87

A Twisted Miser's Tale
Page88

The Bewitching Bog
Page89

Gauntlet of Misdirection
Page90

A Sorcerer's Domain
Page91

The Kingdom at Moonrise
Page92

A Necromancer's Tale
Page93

The Black River of Tears
Page94

Lusters of the Crimson Nectar                    Page95

October 31st is Goth Night
Page96

Sorcery of the Shadow Queen                     Page97

Tales of Morgoth, Lord of Darkness              Page98

Night at the Haunted Bed and Breakfast          Page99

Ruler of the Patch
Page100

**Page 1**

## The Face in the Looking Glass

With my grim eyes, I see a boy, it was the first time I felt love and joy. I may be a goth, but I try to be normal, all bright colors and smiles to look formal. We go on a date till things go awry, now I'm back in the dark with a woeful sigh. But then it turns out, he thought I was cool, so being myself will be my rule. I rise from my foolish mask, showing the confident face for others to bask. The truth was my actual face my actual face, my costumes were all a disgrace. Eye of the tiger and the lion's roar, I was more empowered than never before. My spirits rose to the greatest height, as my inner strength took flight.

**Page2**

### Song of Sorrows

As I listen to music sweet ang tragic, it begins to work its gothic magic. Beauty can come from sadness, as art can be born from one's madness. Grim images fill my mind, at every corner, new inspiration to find. I unleash the darkness of my heart, from it, comes tearful art. Being a goth is not all gore, sometimes, it's so much more. Goths always see the bright side of death, sometimes to see it, you must be out of breath. To become a goth, it doesn't take long, all you need is one soulful song.

**Page3**

## Music from a Darkened Soul

 The gothic music fills the air, unleashing all its frightful flair. As the song plays in the graveyard at night, I look up to the full moonlight. Shining in the shrouding fog, thicker than a swampy bog. Creatures rising from the dead, with a lust for blood and dread. You may make a run for the gate, but they block your exit in a manner so great. Since your escape was a fail, your night will end with a heart-stopping wail.

## Page4

### Metal and Rock

As gothic music gives me a shock, in the forms of heavy metal and rock. I see bats and owls swarming around, their movement then has me spellbound. They fly with the wings of night, as they prowl with peck and bite. Under the stars and full moonlight, the creatures arise to cause a fright. Despite the music being tragic, I get gothic metal and rock work its magic. Magic infused rock is how I roll, as its spell sends me out of control.

**Page5**

<u>Into my Mind</u>

As I split my soul from flesh and bone, I've taken a journey of my own. I have ventured deep into my mind, from within, I begin to unwind. In my trance, I entered a new world, where the line between fantasy and reality is curled.

Sanity and madness, the mental states, both are types of life altering gates. There are many answers you can find; all you must do is enter your mind. Entering the mind is like falling down the rabbit hole, being locked in limbo can take its toll. As one views the subconscious mind, the state of your psyche could either break or bind.

## Beauty of Tragedies

In my book of inspiration, abstract thoughts and emotions begin their manifestation. As I listen to a gothic selection, I expand my poetic collection. Time and time again, I endure endless strife; but music and poetry refills me with life. Gothic style may fill others with fright; but from the darkness, I find peace and light. It may be like living in the night, but it's how my abstract thoughts shine bright. My writing excels to a greater length, for gothic poetry empowers me with inner strength. Confidence and truth become the keys, as I embrace the actual me.

## My Inner Blackness

I discovered a deeper side of my soul; from that, I feel more whole. My subconscious revealed inner blackness, a mind of total darkness. Like the story of "Jekyll & Hyde", I confronted my darker side. From choosing the bat, fearing the maniac and chained door, my mind will be dark and black forevermore. From the darkness; I find my fire, like roar to inspire. My inner strength grows like a flower, with a tiger's eye to help me tower. Confidence and truth became more clearer, as I face the man in mirror.

**Page8**

<u>Art of the Aura</u>

As goth becomes the new fashion, music and art is given a darker passion. Like bats, goths enjoy the night, walking under the ghoulish moonlight. From the void come shrieks and screams, maddening us with bloodcurdling dreams. The big ideas are among the vile, or creepy is the coolest style. I took a deeper look at my chi and saw a cooler reflection of me. My soul is enlightened with magic, by songs of sadness and all that is tragic. My gothic poetry soars to a new length, as it empowers me with inner strength. I make it clear for all to see, that a gothic author is the true me.

**Page9**

## Under the Mask and In the Mirror

Inner strength comes from many places, especially from the reflections of our true faces. Confidence comes not from a mask but a mirror, I knew that lesson couldn't be any clearer. My characters were never the real me, my true persona made it clear to see. My choice to wear a painted face, caused me great shame and disgrace. I decided to be the person I am now, I greeted them with a grin and took a bow. No longer in my silly costumes, accessories or any fancy perfumes.

## Page10

### Poetry of a Madman

Many poets suffered the dark ages, their darker selves escaping their cages. During this old time of sadness, some referred it as divine madness. Creative lunacy sparked like lighters; with artists, musicians and writers. From the tragedy came genius brains, artworks brewed from their mental pains. The black era brought hardship to many hearts; but from the insanity, came true art. But poetry takes me to greater lengths, as it brings me inner strength. I'm empowered like never before, as reading and writing has given me the heart of Gryffindor.

**Page11**

## Journal of a Blackened Heart

From my mind to each page, I write down my pain and rage. To keep my psyche from its brink, my demons are banished to the world of paper and ink. When my life's engulfed in badness, I continue my method of madness. As darkness becomes my inspiration, poetry's my choice of manifestation. As my collection of artistry grows, sweet and silent peace of mind flows. To those of us with black hearts, our escape is the dark arts. From my work, I find inner strength; as confidence and truth allows me to take my skills to a greater length.

**Page12**

### Soul of the Wolf

Like the transformation of "Jekyll and Hyde", I embrace my wild side. The venom gives me inner strength, empowering me to a greater length. As I bathe in the full moonlight, my senses amplify to a new height. My beast escapes its mental cage, as I transform with a mighty rage. My bite's as bad as my bark, for I am a hound of the dark. Based on my dreary life, my view on the world is endless strife. Beware of my powerful growl, as you hear the werewolf's howl.

## The Last Sail of the Sea Ghoul

Ding-dong, the captain's dead, Knock-knock, death is at the door; his arrival means fear and dread forevermore.

The crew panicked with fear so thick, as some of them caught scurvy and got seasick. The crew abandoned ship as it crashed, they headed for the lifeboats and dashed. This was the captain's final trip, as he went down with his ship. Yo-ho-ho, we blew the man down, into the drink, the ship and its captain did drown.

## Page14

### As Bats take Flight

As bats swarm and take fight, Dracula rises from his crypt and to the night. And while his minions cause a fright, mortals pray for morning's first light. For as the sun is shining bright, all vampires must get out of sight. Only at the sun's early light, mortals are safe from Dracula's undead bite.

## Specter of the Darkened Theater

On the organ, I play my song; my grim tune fills the air all night long. I've been forsaken to this horrid place, for no one can handle my disfigured face. They say I'm a monster, a creature of night; my ghostly appearance gives all who gaze a fright. The darkness becomes my domain, a place where I dwell in sorrow and pain. I must lurk in this blackened stage for good, hide my monstrous looks under a cloak and hood.

**Page16**

## Ghosts' Night Out

When phantoms begin the spooking spree, they rise from the grave with ghoulish glee. When the old clock tower strikes at midnight, they begin to cause a horrible fright. For at the stroke of the haunting hour, the specters unleash their ghastly power. They know of what you fear the most, for they haunt your dreams like a ghost.

## Down in Cryptsville

Buried in the blackened ground, where the blowing gusts are the only sound. Sealed within a darkened tomb, I escape from life's doom and gloom. As I take my final breath, I feel the icy grip of death. Once the grim reaper knocks on my door, I am put to rest forevermore. Finding silence will never be hard, once you go to sleep in the graveyard.

**Page 18**

## Secrets of Mystery Island

On an island in the sea, lies all sorts of enigmatic secrets and mystery. What creatures hide within the darkness, and how long have they been in the blackness? What hidden treasures are there to find, protected by the most difficult puzzles of the mind. To my surprise that is tragic, I see the witchdoctor work his voodoo magic. A voodoo priest with amazing power, casting hexes to start the witching hour. You're in for a wild ride, cause the shadow man has friends on the other side!

**Page19**

## Shadows of Grim Jazz

Deep in the fog smoky and thick, lies a shadow slim and slick. There lies a phantom in the night, as fills children up with fright. They say he's black as the night sky, riding on nightmares as they fly. You try to run as fast as you can, but you can't escape the boogeyman! He loves the sound of rolling dice, as he haunts the whole house, even the mice. Children should all take care, or he'll haunt your little nightmares. To make his snake & spider stew so nice; he'll add snails, some slugs and slimy bugs for spice. He gambles and cheats as best as he can, cause he's the bogie boogeyman.

## Terror among the Fields

In the fields on my post, I haunt your dreams like a ghost. I unleash my ghoulish power, as we approach the haunting hour. My powers are capable of quite a scare, as you have the most horrid nightmares. And soon your fear of me will grow, for I am the scarecrow. I'm known as the master of fear, so all must beware my shadow as I appear. He spreads his fear in a cloud of toxic gas, as the nightmare continues until the cloud pass. Only at the stroke of midnight, do mortals find freedom from his tyrannical fright.

## Page21

### Along came a Spider

Once you enter, you can never leave; for the web is where she weaves. When she wields her dark magic, she will cause all events to turn tragic. With darkness like you never seen, all must beware the spider queen! The queen will give you quite a scare, for she lurks in Shelob's lair. The queen is known as mistress of gloom, as she weaves a cobweb of doom. Beware of the queen's blackened heart, for her soul is full of the dark arts! With the colors of purple and black, her spells will cause quite an attack!

**Page22**

## Nightmare under the Big Top

Coney Island is a place void of any frowns, cause it's an island of crazed clowns. AS you listen to the laughter and fear, know that it only comes once a year. Here at the circus of fright, where we only open and perform at night. Come one, come all; to let children of all ages know, beware the looney name of freakshow. Laughter and screams will be the only sounds, as you attend the darkest show around. Entertainment fills the air, as you are given a Spooktacular Scare! As you go along for the ride, you'll find yourself on the other side.

**Page23**

## The Creation of a Monster

In the laboratory of my castle, I work on my experiments without hassle. A creature of both chaos and magic, as starswirl's experiments turned tragic. I build a body without strife as I wait for lightning to give it life. The monster awakens with pure madness, but it came from the creator's sadness. Without worry of his final breath, I create a monster straight from death. This beast of fantastic power created by a wizard's mind shattering hour. Now doomed by this creation of mine, forever to be known as Frankenstein! Centuries passed since that stormy night, but at last the creature has seen the light.

**Page24**

## Boogeyman of the Bayou

The big easy is full of jazz music in the air, but the swamp is where you'll find fear and despair. Witchdoctors working their voodoo magic, casting hexes to make life tragic. Visitors should run and hide or meet the voodoo man's friends on the other side. Swamp monsters and bayou beasts, all coming for the midnight feast. Mardi Gras on bourbon street, the best time for a jazzy retreat. Cajun cooking turns up the heat, burning with dynamite flavor no one can beat. Prepare for scares like you never seen, when you go down to New Orleans.

**Page25**

## The Dark Tales of Comics

I terrorize the city with a shocking scare, as I scheme from my secret lair. Heroes try to take me down, a I commit crimes all over town. They try to put me behind bars, while my name is known wide and far. Being the bad guy is so thrilling, cause a villain's life is bone chilling. The supervillain has all the fun, which is why he's rooted by everyone. When the day can't be saved by superheroes, the bad guys make them look like zeroes. When people want to be the bad guy, the fun begins as dark sparks fly.

## The Spirit of Fright on All Hollow's Night

I am the night of horror and fear, as I come around once a year. I fill the children's hearts with fright, once day turns to maddening night. I unleash my haunting power, when the clock strikes the witching hour. Children beware of the unseen, for it's the night of Halloween! Let all goths may witness, as Halloween claims victory at the arrival of its mistress. Phantoms clanking in rattling chains, condemned for causing others pain. The All Hollow's Queen is in command, now our gothic night is at hand.

**Page27**

## One Good Scare

Pumpkins carved with ghoulish faces, as a small spook hide in many places. With zombies rising from the grave; along with mummies and vampires, you must be brave. As sci-fi scares give you a fright, the monstrous mistress haunts you all night. When you hear a monster's tale, a black sugar cloud hangs overhead as you wail. You might find a twisted treat, but a freak accident is what you'll meet.

Pressure causes a total meltdown, as the final face-off begins the last countdown.

**Page28**

## Under the Tombstone

In the mausoleum, they lie and nest; so, the deceased may have eternal rest. From the crypt on Halloween night, the dead walk the earth to cause a fright. Skeletons rattle with clanking chains, as zombies rise to gobble down brains. Spirits rise in ragged shrouds, as a ghostly fog blows through the clouds. When the gargoyles are on guard, you must beware the old boneyard.

## The Black Granite

My reign of terror is a force no one can block, as I turn my foes into piles of rock. Fear the wrath of me and my pack, as we turn everything pitch black. Our evil will forever have a hold, as everyone turns hard and cold. My dark powers shall chill every single bone, for I have a heart of stone. Beware the blackness I shall bring; for I am Rockwell Blackstone, the Gargoyle King!

## Down for the Final Count

As a ghostly wind blows and moans, all around lie piles of bones. At the tragic end of one's life, the reaper swings his bloody scythe. When the horseman of death knocks on the door, the angels put you to slumber forevermore. Soon we all will rest in peace, when the time comes to join the deceased. When it's time for our final breath, we must depart with our equal and old friend, Death.

## Madame of Blackness

My heart now burns with blackened fire, for I have been bitten by the lord of vampire. The nighttime sky is under my rule, for I'm the monarch over ghastly ghouls. Romance brews as I meet another creature, a dapper creep with gothic chic features. At the time of morning's first light, my minions and I must get out of sight. Mortals are safe from my bloodlust broth, but sundown marks the arrival of the Queen of Goth.

## Two States of the Same Mind

In my lab, I brew my potion; as a dark miracle is set in motion. After one sip, I fall into a deep trance; as horrific visions and nightmarish images sing and dance. I free the madness from my mind, as my suppressed subconscious begins to unwind. I seek out to cause others pain; as I don top hat, cape and cane. Now a member of the dark side, goodbye Henry Jekyll and Hello Edward Hyde!

## Of Two Minds

Like the story of "Jekyll & Hyde", everyone has a light and dark side. On the half of light, purity and the just, to do goodness everywhere is our must. But as for our darker and more unjustly part, we only act out of a stone-cold heart. But throughout our lives, there's a constant battle; causing our minds to shatter and rattle. There're two mental states of a brain, one is a genius and the other's insane. As you look inside your head, you must choose which side will spread.

## When Two Minds become One

As my two minds shake, rattle and roll; my light and darkness fight for control. My dark side tries to escape its mental cage, so it can unleash its powerful rage. But I make a deal bound in chains, to balance my joys with his pains. Now my mind is like a candle, burning at both ends in a way I can handle.

## A Mind split in Two

As I fall into a trance, I give my mind a two-way glance. My inner darkness plays mind games, as my mental state goes up in flames. He grows weary of his cage in my mind, revenge on his captor is what he longs to find. Time after time, he insists; wondering and pondering on why he exists. He volunteers to take control but containing him is how I stay whole. In the end, we both decide, to split the mind and control each side.

## My Dark Reflection

The moon has risen, and day becomes night, now is the time to spread fear and fright. Villainy and crime become my drive, as this curse makes me feel alive. With top hat, cape and cane in hand, I shall spread horror throughout the land. Crazed with a desire to terrorize the neighborhood, driven to destroy all that is good. My kinder half is locked away, never again to see the light of day. Sinister as the darker side, for all shall beware the name of Hyde! Tonight, and forever, I'll raise the dark side, For I am Mr. Edward Hyde.

## The Ways of You-Know-Who

With serpentine spells and skeletal wands, witches and dark wizards make blackened bonds. The Dark Lord casts his signature curse, as *Descente Tenebro* makes everything worse. Wisdom of owls and cruelty of crows, as they do things no one wants to know. *The Puzzling Hex* unhinges your mind, confusing it till it unwinds. Potions and spellbooks on the cases, as dark wizards laugh with crooked smirks on their faces. *Gothicus Glacius* starts a grim winter, as *Congelos Metuos* stings like a splinter. When the clock strikes the witching hour, mortals beware of their dark power. *Emittia Vesania* unleases madness, as *Tenebrum Autum* ensure a fall season of badness.

**Page38**

### Emperor of Entropy

To others, I bring mental pain, as *Chausa Celebra* drives everyone insane. *Emittia Vesania* cause minds to shatter, my spell shall drive you mad as a hatter. I spread chaos and lunacy all around, making every great mind to go unsound. Laughter fills the air, as screwloose spells beginning beyond compare. My magic is capable of reaching all, turning them all into screwballs. I unleash all that is sick and wrong, as all falls under the chaos song. As my lament plays on in my mind, a missing piece proves to be something I must find. No one is a match for the Chaos Lord, for I am known by the name of Discord!

## Hands and Sands

Tick tock, tick tock; it's time to check on the clock. I am the one unstoppable power; for I know every second, minute and hour. I am everywhere far and near; for I know every day, week, month and year. From back in the past to what the future beholds; one at a time, I allow them to unfold. What's not known about the grim reaper, he is the ultimate timekeeper. I make sure things happen on the dime, for I am the hands and sands of time. As the sands run out in your hourglass, the time has come for you to pass. I am the never-ending rhyme, for I am the force known as time.

### The Grand Duke of Night

Tweedle-le-de, tweedle-le-do; the Duke of Darkness is after you! Tweedle-le-de, tweedle-le-ding; beware as he flies through the skies with darkened wings. Tweedle-le-de, tweedle-le-ding; beware the most horrific owl you've ever seen. Tweedle-le-de, tweedle-le-doe; he partners up with blackbirds, ravens and crows. Tweedle-le-de, tweedle-delight; the Duke of Darkness rules the night! Tweedle-le-de, tweedle-le-duel; the Duke is master of ghosts and ghouls. Tweedle-le-de, tweedle-le-down; the Duke is who wears the blackness crown! Tweedle-le-de, tweedle-le-dye; beware for he rules the sky.

## Howl of the Hound

At the rising of the full moon, the wolfbane flowers blossom and bloom. As lycanthropy takes total control, the curse of the werewolf will take its toll. Alpha, Beta and Omega, the howling three; enough to cause a biting spree. Creatures that are half-man and half-beast, arising to the night for a feast. In the darkest woods, they hunt when they can, so beware of the wolfman.

### The Isle of No Escape

On an island at the heart of the Bermuda Triangle, lived a sea witch with lochs of hair in a nasty tangle. Her pirate of a daughter rules the shore, where visitors stay forevermore. She sails the seas as a black-hearted buccaneer, swashbuckling as she spreads pain and fear. The crew recites the serpent's tale, sea stories to make sailors wail. No one is safe from her grip, once you see her at the helm of her ship. The Water Wand, her pirate boat; navy men scream as she gloats. Seahag Suzie be her name, fear it; for plundering and looting is her game.

## Welcome to the House of Bio-Exorcism

In this house, you must be wary; still welcome to a place where all is gothic and scary. Ghostly hauntings occurring every night, as the whole family fills to the brim with fright. It's showtime with every scare, as ghoulish organ music fills up the air. The entire house flows with gloom and depression, as haunted items are caused by ghastly possession. Shadows rise up every resident, even the mouse; one you enter this haunted house. Taboo occurs when you say the ghost's name 3 times, because you'll be exposed to all his creepy crimes. All who enter will fall and burn, for no one can escape the house of no return.

## Legends beyond the Grave

A dark legend with a wicked spell to cast, as we speak of the greatest villains of history's past. Fire burns within your eyes, as you make the best of the worst rise. With the voodoo staff in hand, we summon villains small and grand. Slithering snakes plot and scheme, as they bring to life their monstrous dream. From the volcano, the legend shall rise, ready to give the world a horrific surprise.

## Pleasant Dreams, Pleasant Screams

As gothic music plays on in my head, heavy metal and rock fills me with dread. Nights of macabre and hours of horror, as my slumber fills with terror. My dreams turn dark and cold, what nightmarish monsters will my imagination behold? The boogeyman haunts my dreams like a ghost, for he knows what scares me the most. Nightmares from my subconscious coming to life, a power to spread endless strife.

## The Dark Side of Imagination

I close my eyes and say goodnight, as stars gleam, and the moon shines bright. But outside rages a thunderstorm, then my greatest fears began to swarm. A creature comes into my sight, the look of it gave me a fright. I ran for my life as my heart skips a beat, hearing the monster's stomping feet. The beast chased me all over the bog, as I tried to lose it in the fog. I awaken with a shocking scare, only to discover it was just a nightmare.

## My Dark Oz

Deep within the 4$^{th}$ dimension, lies a construx beyond all comprehension. Everything causes my brain to scatter, driving me mad as a hatter. As the Chaos Lord leads me to wonderland's door, I envisioned discord's madness and more. The air fills up with Halloween Jazz, making you a total spazz. Hear this and hear it well, enter limbo and you'll fall under its crazed spell.

## A Dark and Snowy Night

At the beginning of a dark and cold night, when all is pitch black and snowy white. A powerful storm blows a frosty breeze, as the icy winds cause all to freeze. Storm clouds shower and hail, as the wind gives a moaning wail. Hardening icicles make a shimmering sound, as all becomes icebound. When all solidifies in place, a gust of frost will blow into your face. The chill on your back will sting like a splinter, for no one can withstand a gothic winter.

## A Blue Day

When I have a bad day, my misfortunes fill me with sorrow and dismay. As a dark cloud hangs over my head, weakness and sadness begin to spread. From every corner, I got stuck, I kept ending up with rotten luck. On every Friday the 13$^{th}$, I always end up underneath. My only forecast is gray rain, as my sadness spreads with my pain. Gloomy moans are all I can say, because I was having a bad day.

## Counting down the All Hollow's Clock

As the countdown to Halloween begins, now come contests and competitions to win. Ghoulish magic turning loose; like Jack, Elder Gutknecht, Harry and Beetlejuice. Lord Voldemort and Mr. Oogie Boogie frighten kids the dark arts, causing nightmares and breaking hearts. Spells to cast and treats to snatch, as Hagrid works in Jack's pumpkin patch. There's much for Dumbledore and Skellington to weave, as Hogwarts and Halloween Town prepare for All Hollow's Eve.

## Screams at Storytime

From my mind to what I write, my poetic skills spread horrific delight. With pens of black and red ink, I shock you with the darkest fantasy that I can think. Many authors try their hand, writing tales and poems to spread classic horror throughout the land. Some base their work on the gothic lifestyle, as they spread terror for miles and miles. Ghost and supernatural stories that were constantly told, each one was written in the dark ages of old. The gothic tradition of literary horror, all started with Mary Shelby's tale of terror.

## My Perilous Place

In many places around the earth, legends of horror were given birth. From Stanley hotel to Bran Castle, ghosts appear and cause a hassle. Even from in the White House, presidents of the past stirred up everyone, even a mouse. From Salem to Transylvania, many places are prime for the monster mania. Graveyards, manors and castles, oh my; as the settings cause the darkest of fantasies to fly. Creepy inns and haunted towns, enough to turn smiles into frightened frowns. Beware all who visits a tomb, or just might seal your doom. Ghouls will appear before your faces as you visit the world's scariest places.

## Zoo of the Nocturnal

Here inside our possessed nocturnal zoo, the only prey will be you! Explore our exhibits of rats, they might be under your floor mats. Our hyenas laugh and grimly grin all night, when they find something for them to bite. Next come our swarms of bats, along with our display of black cats. Then we have our wolves, our howling hounds; their growl causes new horror to become unbound. Finally, we show our ravens, blackbirds, crows and owls; birds of darkness oh so fowl! Our zoo will give you a primal fright, as you see the creatures of the night.

## Nursery of Nightmares

Laughing Jack and Laughing Jill, who both climbed up a haunted hill. They looked for a well to fill their pail but found something that made them wail. They found a black and white big top, with a sight to make jaws drop. Inside the tent at the center ring, stood painted faces that dance and sing. Jack and Jill joined in that night, as the cursed circus disappeared at morning's first light. Now as members of the dark carnival, their lives will be an endless black festival.

### Fiendish Fools

We spread madness throughout our towns, for we are crazed crime clowns. From the prankster to the jester, known to tease and mock with every gesture. From Mr. Mxyptlk to the trickster, a pair of screwballs to play the slicksters. Finally comes the prince of poker, he's known only as the Joker! Oh, how we love to commit crimes, battling superheroes are such wonderful times! We cause chaos with twisted styles, crazed laughter and mad smiles. Joke-themed villains are so much fun, trying to get a laugh out of everyone.

## Bloodsucker's Ball

In Transylvania, the vampires dance, as bats arise to the night and start to prance. From the ballroom of Bran Castle, Dracula's undead dinner party causes quite a hassle. After the party, they fly to the bat sanctuary, where mortals should all be wary. As Chiroptophobia fills the air, Dracula's organ song plays everywhere! Finally, comes the vampire graveyard, where Van Helsing sends his prey, but sends them hard.

## Phantoms of Mardi Gras

Down in the Big Easy at night, ghosts arise to cause a terrible fright. First, we have the Chapel of the glass eye, where spooks awaken and fly. Next comes the St. Louis cemetery, with above ground tombs to make it extra scary. All ruled by the Voodoo Queen, with things you never want to be seen. St. Louis is the city of the dead, so try not to lose your head! In the city of lost souls, no ghost is truly whole. The Shadow Man can take you for a ride, with help from his friends on the other side.

## Old Wicked West

Down in the wild west, where outlaws ride in to bring out everyone's worst and best. The posse rides on horseback into town, they look around as the sun went down. They arrive and head to the saloon, the outlaw and his goons. At the poker table, the gang all band; as the outlaw plays a dead man's hand. The sheriff calls out the outlaw and goons, for a showdown at high noon. At the stand-off, the townsfolk prepare for the worst; wondering who will fire first. At the stroke of high noon, they fire at will; now the sheriff and the outlaw both rest at boot hill.

## Last Ride at Sundown

Down in the old town of Tombstone, rode in a ghoulish ranger of bones. At the rising of the moon, the ranger heads over to the saloon. Over at the saloon, he playeda game quite grand; as he deals out a dead man's hand. He was caught cheating by the sheriff of the town, who challenged him to a showdown. At the heart of town, the men wait uintil midnight;wondering who will start the fight. When they fired, all went still; for both men are now sleeping at boot hill.

## Elemental Darkness

Throughout the age, each day and night; there were forces of darkness and light. Forces battle and conspire, angelic bliss and demonic fire. Spirit animals of the lion and the snake, a war to cause the earth and heaven to quake. Light magic and the Dark arts; when choosing your side, you must be kind, brave and smart. In the colors of red and green, kindness and cruelty like you never seen. This battehas been going on for the ages, recorded in the history pages.

## Winter Terrorland

As Jack Frost nips at everyone's nose, a stormy dark and cold wind blows. The icy winds blow a mighty breeze, as the world is given a wicked freeze. Cold and dark becomes the night, as all is turned blue and white. Heed this warning and remember, this frozen nightmare always begins in December. Selfish magic brings endless snow, for a cold heart can never grow.

## A Spell from Down Below

As witches send spells confounding my mind, confusion and illusion causes me to unwind. Sorcerers brew potions from their books of spells, planning to trick us oh so quite well. Magicians using the power of illusion; causing chaos, confoundment and confusion. Warlocks wielding the darkest of magic, forbidden practices to make all grim and tragic. Masters of blackness try to fool you, so beware when they work their voodoo. On Halloween Night with a plot to hatch, they prepare the witchcraft of old scratch.

## Khristmas of Krampus

*Gruss vom Krampus* is their final phrase, as naughty children endure endless snow days. He'll play every Christmas trick, so beware the shadow of old St Nick. Krampus' punishment is what he'll insist, so kids must try to be good and stay off his naughty list. Beware all you bad girls and boys, or you'll deserve Krampus' toys. You must allow the spirit to thrive, or you won't escape when Krampus arrives. As cold winds blow on a dark winter's night, out goes all of the candlelight. For kids who misbehaved all year long, you'll only sing along to krampus' song. At the sound of the ringing bells, Krampus and his helpers cast their spell.

## My Raging Elemental

Deep from within my mind lives a fiery darkness, forged by my anger to a powerful blackness. Locked away from within my own head, lies a maddening and scorching shade of red. My inner darkness is my greatest fear, as his hot-headed fire burns all far and near. He frees himself when I need him the most, but he lurks in my nightmares like a ghost. His blistering blaze is a flamming fate, for he is anger incarnate.

## Little Store of Nightmares

In the Dark Carnival and all it's features; lies oddballs, freakshows and other creatures. As the Dark Carnival plays its sound, perpare for the darkest show around. Creatures to spread delight or horror, some can cause fantasy or terror. This Festival of Blackness comes once a year, on Halloween to spread your deepest and darkest fear. Some creatures are fun and others cause a fright, creatures of day and others of the night. Only goths may enter and survive, for those who criticize them will never thrive. Creatures horrifying enough to make your heart stop, so beware when you enter the Big Top.

## Council of Gothlords

Masters of *malice* and *hazard*, cold and dark a wicked wizard. Masters of *misery* and *fear*, spreading gloom and melancholy far and near. Masters of *plague* and *pain*, spreading sickness to shatter a brain. In the Grand Council Hall, the Elders of Gothlore plot the Lords of Order's downfall. The Dark Lord sits as chairman of the board, as his followers plan their acts of discord. As the Half-Blood Prince arrives at the meeting, he joins into this grim greeting. They plan to attack at the midnight hour, to win the war with the blackest of power.

## A Wayward Land

Down the rabbit hole we fall, where madness reigns from wall to wall. Through the rhyming words we tumble, where brains scatter and mentality crumbles. When people ask me what's the matter, my answer i that I'm mad as the hatter. All is nonsense in a world where time doesn't exist, where contrary wisdom is what everyone insist. As everyone ties to change your state of mind, you're locked in a limbo where psyches unwind. When the soul shatters in pain, all sanity is removed from the brain. Once you're out of your head, you'll find yourself dreaming in bed.

**Page68**

## Nocturnal Horror

At moonrise when the moment is nigh, starlight glimmers and fills up the sky. When moonshine covers the land, a nightmare begins oh so grand. Villainous music plays in the air, with nightly terror beyond compare. Moonlighting on Halloween night, full of creatures to cause a fiendish fright. Monsters, horrors and terrors of night; snarling, growling and ready to bite. All Hollow's Eve is a ghoulish night, as witchcraft and wizardry brings upon a ghastly delight.

**Page69**

## The Forsaken Island

Ghost Island is the home of Lord BlackSpell, the Prince of Necromancers; with zombies and skeletons as his voodoo dancers. On this island, a weighty choice is yours to make, you could choose the right selection or a big mistake. But if the wrong decision you choose to do, then your choice will forever haunt you. Ghost Island is full of ghouls, some are screwball specters and others are fiendish fools. Lord BlackSpell lives in a volcanic castle, riddled with enough traps to cause quite a hassle. So choose wisely as you make your selection, or Lord BlackSpell will add your soul to his collection.

**Page70**

## The Silent Face of Tragedy

My painted face wears a black frown, for I am the opposite of a clown. All is black and white and sometimes gray, for I wear these colors all day. I never make a single sound, as move my arms and legs all around. Never silenced in theaters both far and near, as I face the audience with painted tears. Everything I gesture comes to life, comedies full of hope and tagedies full of strife. Every hour is quiet time, for I am as silent as a mime.

## The Goblin Hour of Night

As the sun goes down on Halloween Night, goblins arise to cause a blood-curdling fright. Halloween jazz and gothic music fills the air, as goblins creep around and have some fun with an unnerving scare. When the clock strikes the witching hour, the goblin king unleashes his wizarding power. Some live in caves and others in spooky towns, some goblins even work as dark carnival clowns. Goblins have so much mischief to weave, when it's time for All Hollow's Eve.

## Dark Justice

I am the terror among crime lords at night, filling criminals and lawbreakers with fright. From a cloud of smoke and I appear, for my greatest weapons are mystery and fear. Villains ask and wonder about this and that, as they see the shadow of the bat. I'm a nightmare who will do well, punishing lawbreakers with my mysterious spell. My darkwings allowed me to fly, as criminals feared my shadow soaring in the midnight sky. I'm known as a master detector, for I am the Black Inspector.

A Harmonious Hex

As we begin to play magic infused rock, our song will charge you with a scaring shock. Our feet slam down on the pedal, as we start rocking out our heavy metal. My guitar is my staff with the magic of the drums and keyboard, casting musical spells and symphonic discord. Every note is played with fire, for musical magic is our one desire. Our symphonic spell will put you under our command, because we are a bewitching rock band.

**Page74**

<u>Bewitched by the BoogeyWoman</u>

As my cauldron starts to bubble, I prepare to hex up some trouble. With shadows, bats and a sorcerous surprise; I'll cast my spell and you won't believe your eyes. My broomstick and wand are in my hands, so I can spread my necromanic jinx throughout the land. Once you pay the toll and sign the scroll, it's there when you sell me your soul. My necromancy will make you twitch, for I am a wicked witch.

## Wraith of the Witchdoctor

The priest of voodoo works his black magic, a jazzy force so dark and tragic. But meets a hero brave and true, ruining his plans through and through. So the shadow man plots his revenge, a wrath as hard as the rocks of Stonehenge. He summons his friends on the other side, sending our hero on a wild ride. But the hero continues to end his crimes, so their rivalry is sealed for all of time.

## The Black Palace

Within my hallowed halls, spirits rise and dance at my grand balls. As the organ music fills the air, shadows arise to cause quite a shocking scare. Vampires, werewolves and other spooks; causing great fear and spreading nightmares with crazed kooks. Darkness flows from throne room to hall, as blackness riegns from wall to wall. Creatures of dark and cold power, skulking and lurking in every tower. The afterlife is a horrific hassle, here inside Lord BlackSpell's haunted castle.

## His Royal Horrificness

From within my castle of darkness, I rule a kingdom of pitch blackness. Through the shadowy halls I stumble, where courage collapses and crumble. Ravens, crows and blackbirds fly over the pumpkin patch, with spooky faces to mix and match. Vampires and the undead at every twist and turn, with lusts for blood and magic to burn. There's much terror and horror to bring; for I am Griswald Gothicus, the apparition king.

## A Spooktacular Sundown

As the sun sets and the moon rises up high, stars bedazzle in the darkened sky. Colors of black, purple and blue; shine in the darkness through. Nocturnal beasts begin to awake, a frightful sight to make you shiver and shake. The air fills up with all kinds of dreams, some with laughter and others with screams. You might encounter creatures of the unseen, especially on the night of Halloween. I'm telling you it's quite a fright, of what goes on when day becomes night.

## Lord of the Unliving

The Underworld is a land of dread, where I rule as lord of the dead. Charon ferries on the river styx, so prepare pay the ferryman without any tricks. Cerberus gaurds over the unseen; as I rule with Persephone, my underworld queen. Darkness and gloom spreads all around, for I rule a kingdom underground. Fear my flames gentlemen and ladies; for I am the greek god of death, Hades.

**Page81**

## The Dark Baron of Bats

I am the vengeance of the night, bringing terror with my undead bite. People wonder if they saw black cats, but all they see are shadows of the bat. Mortals fear the sight of my scowl, with my eyebrows arched like that of an owl. With fangs and a heart of blsck fire, beware the curse of the vampire. Bloodsuckers with a grim tune to sing; all rise for Count Dracula, the Vampire King.

**Page82**

<u>Shades and Contrasts of Night</u>

Dark as the night sky over a meadow; I am Mortimer Darkshade, the king of shadows. I'm the blackest shadow in the darkest night, as I'm cast on the full moonlight. One second, I arrive and in the next, I disappear; for I can be everywhere far and near. My land is black, white and gray; where it's always night and never day. Gloom and doom is my prance, as my shadow puppets do my phantasmic dance.

Frightmare Night

Every year on October 31st, spirits arise cast their haunting curse. Samhainophobics cower in fear, as nightmare come from far and near. Bats and owls all take flight, as they soar on this ghoulish night. It's a night of tricks and treats, full of spooky scares and tasty sweets. Creatures wake with ghastly glee, when they begin the midnight haunting spree. Halloween night will give you a scare, so have fun in your worst nightmare.

**Page84**

## The Origin of a Dark Professor

Riddle me this, riddle me that: who's the villain under the thinking cap? He believes to have the world's greatest mind, the smartest criminal to ever find. Knowledge is true power, his intelligence causes heroes to cripple and cower. He's the genius of the dark arts, a brilliant mind with a blackened heart. His brain is greater than any processor; for I am Edward Sprocketworx, the crazed professor.

Chiroptophobia

From the forms of dwarves to dolls, they stalk and lurk in the shadowy halls. With wings to fly and fangs to bite, they allow their bloodlust to take flight. Bloodsuckers of the ice and red, their enchanting presence fills us with dread. With shadows of bats and hearts of black fire, there's no creature darker than the vampire.

## Shades of Blackened Blue

Deep within my mind, the gothic face of tragedy is all I can find. Gloom and doom both far and near, reducing me to a river of tears. A list of problems either short or steep, enough to make me cry and weep. So, when the world is grim and full of badness, sometimes it helps to feel sadness. Life isn't always a comedy of errors, sometimes, it's a tregedy of terrors. Life leaves me overstressed, so I'll create gothic literature from being depressed.

**Page87**

## Shades of Darkened Purple

I can endure your mental pains, as life plays it's twisted mind games. As gothic music plays its eerie sound, many dangers lurk all around. My imagination lets my nightmares go free, as they start a maddening spree. Masters of horror and terror lurk in my dreams, filling the air with my screams. Anxiety and dread are never a breeze; as we fight, flight or freeze. Pobias are there and here, so, it never hurts to feel fear.

## A Twisted Miser's Tale

I never had fun and laughter throughout my life, it was nothing but endless darkness and strife. Some say I have a bent up soul, it's true that my heart has a hole. It's true my morals are pitch black, for my point of view is a cruel attack. As a storm rages outside my crooked house; all creaures stir, even a crooked mouse. There's no philosophy darker than mine, which I find simply divine. I act as unscrupulous as I can, for I am a crooked man.

## The Bewitching Bog

Spook Swamp is the home of Marsha Grimsley, the horrible hag; haunting the bayou with her magic bag. Herbs and spices for her witch's brew; with spellbooks, potions and artifacts to work her voodoo. Stem of mushroom and head of toadstool, unleash witchcraft black and cruel. Black marshes swampy and boggy, full of air thick and foggy. The witching hour is finally right, so I'll haunt my land with horror and fright.

## Gauntlet of Misdirection

You can't always trust your eyes, you'll be doomed for a big surprise. Magicians perform amazing feats, wonderful tricks as your treats. Jesters make nothing as it seems, their illusions are their forms of your dreams. Tricksters try to twist the truth, telling lies that are untrue and uncouth. Some are comical and others are tragic, for there's two sides when it comes to magic. Delusions can alter one's perception, for that is the power of deception.

**Page91**

## A Sorcerer's Domain

Deep within a fantastic castle, things to figure out can be quite a hassle. My castle decor is all gothic and fancy, as I work on my magic and necromancy. The most sorcerous of arts and other enchanting feats, mastering all sorts of tricks and treats. Forces of the comical and tragic, to bring light and darkness with its magic. Celtic magic dark and light, powers to make all grim or bright. From these practices came a tradition, for mortals are powerless against a magician.

The Kingdom at Moonrise

As negative voltage sparks the sky, dark horses spread their wings and flight. Fast as lightning and black as the night, they spread fear as they take flight. Thestrals of electric darkness, soaring above with shocking blackness. Energized by the nightshade, we watch as the setting sunlight fade. Their speed is beyond compare, as they fly around while giving a scare. Their lunar energy blasts like a volt, for no one can outfly the Shadowbolts.

**A Necromancer's Tale**

With the Seer Wand in my hand, magic and sorcery are at my commands. Dark and light magic flows in the air, witchcraft and wizardry beyond compare. Trained students from Miss Cacklington's School of Magic, learn to balance the comical and tragic. Students learn to become great mages; as the headmistress uses the Wand of Existence, the most powerful wand in history's pages. With a mystical gem as the core, the students take on Lord BlackSpell and the Elders of Gothlore. As the next generation grew, our hero's journey begins anew.

## The Black River of Tears

As sounds of sobbing fill the sky, rain clouds and storms bring me reasons to cry. Whispers of a gusty winter, stinging us like an icy splinter. Roses of black and of red, breaking m heart with each tear I shed. With the tragic face of a creeper, noe can avoid the tears of the weeper.

**Page95**

<u>Lusters of the Crimson Nectar</u>

Wings and shadows of the bat, bewitched by the charms of a black cat. Creatures of the baroque style, rising to the night with a fanged smile. Ruled by a black king and a red queen, they spread horror and fantasy every Halloween. Goths all play their parts, to enchant souls and blacken hearts. The twilight hour brings us wonder and dread, for midnight is the hour of the undead. With a heart of black fire; beware of Count Dracula, the king vampire.

October 31st is Goth Night

As witches perpare the shadow brew, autumn magic formed as its power grew. Pumpkins shine with a spooky smile, grinning in the most fantastic of styles. Rising at midnight from the old boneyard, skeletons and zombies awake cold and hard. By the bite of the werewolf or vampire, come ghoulish tales around the campfire. I play with my voodoo dolls, pulling strings one and all. Hauntings occur both far and near, on this one night of the year. In our town of the unseen, we come out to celebrate Halloween. There's much dark magic to weave, for the night of goths is All Hollows Eve.

## Sorcery of the Shadow Queen

Sealed within a magic coin, only til the eclipse allows my shadow to join. Revenge is now at hand, as my shadow puppets take over the land. To help my wicked plan fly, I created a shadow to act as my spy. But once my staff breaks and shatter, all of my dark powers start to scatter. However, I'll plan my next attack well, for they haven't heard the last of Magica De Spell.

## Tales of Morgoth, Lord of Darkness

Morgoth is one of the many Dark Lords, masters of blackness and discord. Casting the shadow of his mind, within lies much misery to find. As he conquered middle-earth, a new age of darkness begins its birth. He steals a jewel before he weds; if he becomes king, there'll be tranny and dread. By his former servant; Sauron, Morgoth's legacy will go on.

**Page99**

## Night at the Haunted Bed and Breakfast

Come over and spend the night, you'll be in for a terrible fright. In here; we serve breakfast in bed, after a fight night of mystery and dread. With wolves and vamps; ghouls and a ghost, I will be your monstrous host. Spooktacular things for you to see, here at our fantastic B+B. Prepare for a batty surprise; cause once you spend the night, you won't believe your eyes.

**Ruler of the Patch**

I rule over Halloween town, for I wear the jack-o-lantern crown. I can give anyone a good scare, even ghost hunters must beware. In the form of a scarecrow, my nightmares begin as my pumpkin fire starts to glow. I could be lurking in the woods, or I'm terrorizing neighborhoods. On Halloween night; there's horror to bring, for I'm the only Pumpkin King.

### Land of Pitch Black

The Dark Lord and his cult prepare the ritual; an incantation cold, dark and spiritual. Lord BlackSpell and the Elders of Gothlore, their powers will cause joy to spread nevermore. A jinx to cast the land into forever night, as dark wizards cause a terrible fright. The dark mark appears in the sky, as the spell is cast in a battle cry. Followers come to their master's side, spreading his rule far and wide. Lord BlackSpell casts his hex at the witching hour, as the wizarding world fall under his power.

Made in the USA
Middletown, DE
07 October 2020